Exerc... ...

Written by Jo Windsor
Illustrated by Clive Taylor

Training Schedule for Geese

MORNING	How to find good food – slugs, fish, grass
6:00	
	How to waddle
	How to paddle and dive
8:00	
9:00	
AFTERNOON	How to fly
	How to land
1:00	Learning about dangers and how to fly away quickly
2:00	
4:00	Nest time
6:00	

Schedule - Dog Day Care Center

AM	Meeting dogs
7:30	Snack for big dogs
8:00	Snack for little dogs
8:05	Exercise time
9:00-11:00	Lunch
12:00	
PM	Shampoo poodles
1:00	Trim long-haired dogs
2:00	Walks for all dogs
3:00-4:30	Pick up time
4:30-5:00	

Henri's Beauty Shop Appointments

Today : Monday, July 3

AM

9:00	Mr. Mel – Cut and Curl
9:30	(Free time)
10:00	Sales Person
10:30	Mrs. Jack – Braid *Wants pink ribbons and blue and green beads in braids*
11:00	Sweep up and clean shop
12:00	Lunch

PM

1:00	Color for Zack *Change hair color*
2:30	Eyelash Curl – Kate
3:00	Paint Nails – Sasha
4:00	Clean up shop

Machine Schedule
Monday, March 29

AM

9:00	Boot Cleaning Machine
10:00	Teeth Cleaning Machine
11:00	Floor Cleaning Machine
12:00	Milkshake Making Machine

PM

1:00	Dusting Machine
2:00	Hair Curling Machine
3:00	Moustache Trimming Machine

Pet Store Schedule

9:00 am	Feed the fish.
10:00 am	Talk to the parrot.
11:00 am	Clean the mice and rats' cage. (Yuck!)
12:00 noon	Feed the small animals. *(Watch fingers.)*
1:00 pm	Put the warm light on for the turtle. Check he has new fish to chase.
2:00 pm	Exercise the spiders. *(Keep Harry and Bob apart, as they fight.)*
3:00 pm	Check the snake eggs. Some may have hatched. Maybe more food needed.
4:00 pm	Cuddle the kittens.

Hello, I'm Mr. Long. I am a geese trainer. I train young geese that have no parents to look after them. They have to learn how to feed and paddle. They have to learn how to swim and dive, too. I wrote a training schedule to follow. If I follow the schedule, I can make sure that my geese will learn well.

Training Schedule
for Geese

MORNING

6:00   **How to find good food – slugs, fish, grass**

8:00   **How to waddle**

9:00   **How to paddle and dive**

AFTERNOON

1:00   **How to fly**

2:00   **How to land**

4:00   **Learning about dangers and how to fly away quickly**

6:00   **Nest time**

Hi, Mrs. Dilly here. I run a Dog Day Care Center. My center has full day care for all kinds of dogs. I have a schedule set up to plan things that keep the dogs happy and healthy while they stay at the center. My dogs get a choice of balls, toys, socks or old tee-shirts to play with. Old dogs have special sleeping corners in the yard. My staff are very kind people. They keep the dogs happy until their owners pick them up.

Schedule -
Dog Day Care Center

AM

7:30	Meeting dogs
8:00	Snack for big dogs
8:05	Snack for little dogs
9:00-11:00	Exercise time
12:00	Lunch

PM

1:00	Shampoo poodles
2:00	Trim long-haired dogs
3:00-4:30	Walks for all dogs
4:30-5:00	Pick up time

Hello to you all. I'm Mr. Henri. I have the best beauty shop in town. It is a very busy place. I have many people who want to be beautiful. I write the times for them to see me in my appointment book.

Henri's Beauty Shop Appointments

Today : Monday, July 3

AM

9:00	**Mr. Mel – Cut and Curl**
9:30	**(Free time)**
10:00	**Sales Person**
10:30	**Mrs. Jack – Braid** *Wants pink ribbons and blue and green beads in braids*
11:00	**Sweep up and clean shop**
12:00	**Lunch**

PM

1:00	**Color for Zack** *Change hair color*
2:30	**Eyelash Curl – Kate**
3:00	**Paint Nails – Sasha**
4:00	**Clean up shop**

Hello, I'm Mr. Leroy. I make fantastic machines. I sell my machines at shopping malls everywhere. I love it when people try out my machines. Today I have a very busy schedule. I am showing a different machine every hour.

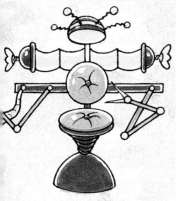

Machine Schedule
Monday, March 29

AM	
9:00	Boot Cleaning Machine
10:00	Teeth Cleaning Machine
11:00	Floor Cleaning Machine
12:00	Milkshake Making Machine
PM	
1:00	Dusting Machine
2:00	Hair Curling Machine
3:00	Moustache Trimming Machine

I'm Ernie. I love ostriches. I live next door to an ostrich farm. After school I help with the ostriches. The farm is a very busy place with new chicks hatching. We have to feed, clean, and exercise the birds. I have a schedule. Each day I have something different to do. I like Wednesday and Thursday the best!

Schedule for Week

	MONDAY	TUESDAY
	Feed ostriches. Look at eggs.	Clean cage #2.

WEDNESDAY	**THURSDAY**	**FRIDAY**
Exercise ostriches.	Take ostriches for a paddle.	Clean cage #1.

Hello, I'm Emily. I own a pet store. I have all kinds of different animals for sale in my store. Everyday there are different jobs to do. I have to keep the pets happy and healthy while they wait in the store for people to buy them. I have a job schedule on my store wall.

Pet Store Schedule

9:00 am	Feed the fish.
10:00 am	Talk to the parrot.
11:00 am	Clean the mice and rats' cage. (Yuck!)
12:00 noon	Feed the small animals. (Watch fingers.)
1:00 pm	Put the warm light on for the turtle. Check he has new fish to chase.
2:00 pm	Exercise the spiders. (Keep Harry and Bob apart, as they fight.)
3:00 pm	Check the snake eggs. Some may have hatched. Maybe more food needed.
4:00 pm	Cuddle the kittens.

Hello! I'm Mr. Roger. I do different things to make people laugh. I play tricks, tell jokes, and read funny stories. I have a very busy schedule.

My "Make People Laugh" Schedule

MONDAY

TUESDAY

WEDNESDAY

Birthday party at 12 Hilly Road Lane, 24 children – Party for Jon.

Visit zoo. Hyenas need cheering up. Zookeeper worried.

Barbecue at the beach. Fun in the sand!

THURSDAY

Visit Senior Citizens' Home – only jokes and stories (no tricks).

FRIDAY

Mrs. Pink's 100th birthday. Wants lots and lots of laughs!

SATURDAY

All day Circus School. Training clowns in laughing and tricks.

Schedules

Purpose:

to plan the things for the day, the week, the month, the year

How to Make a Schedule:

Step One
Think about:

- Why am I making this schedule?
- What is the schedule for?
- What things do I want on the schedule?

Step Two
Write a name for your schedule and write down the things you want on it.

Things to Do on Saturday

soccer
read
walk the dog
see my friends
feed the cat

Step Three
Write down the times you want to do each thing, like this:

Things to Do on Saturday

10:00am	soccer
6:00pm	read
8:00am	walk the dog
2:00pm	see my friends
9:00am	feed the cat

(Make sure you allow enough time to do each thing.)

Step Four
Now put the things on your schedule in the right order.

Things to Do on Saturday

8:00am	walk the dog
9:00am	feed the cat
10:00am	soccer
2:00pm	see my friends
6:00pm	read

Guide Notes

Title: **Exercise Time**
Stage: Fluency (2)

Text Form: Schedules
Approach: Guided Reading
Processes: Thinking Critically, Exploring Language, Processing Information
Written and Visual Focus: Schedules, Speech Bubbles

THINKING CRITICALLY
(sample questions)
- Why do you think Mrs. Dilly has to be at work early?
- Why do you think the appointment for Zack has to be one-and-a-half hours long?
- What day do you think would be the busiest day for Ernie at the ostrich farm?
- Look at the pet store schedule. Which job would you find the most interesting? Why?

EXPLORING LANGUAGE

Terminology
Spread, author and illustrator credits, ISBN number

Vocabulary
Clarify: schedule, trainer, braid, exercise, trimming, appointment
Nouns: geese, fish, dogs, lunch
Verbs: clean, walk, cut, fly
Singular/plural: slug/slugs, goose/geese, person/people
Abbreviations: am (before noon), pm (after noon)

Print Conventions
Dash, colon, apostrophes – possessive (Senior Citizens' Home, Mrs. Pink's 100th birthday, rats' cage), contraction (I'm)
Parenthesis: (Yuck!), (Watch fingers.)

Phonological Patterns
Focus on short and long vowel **a** (sn**a**ck, h**a**ppy, r**a**t, pl**a**ce, c**a**ge)
Discuss root words – beautiful, making, trimming, worried
Look at suffix **ly** (quick**ly**), **y** (health**y**)